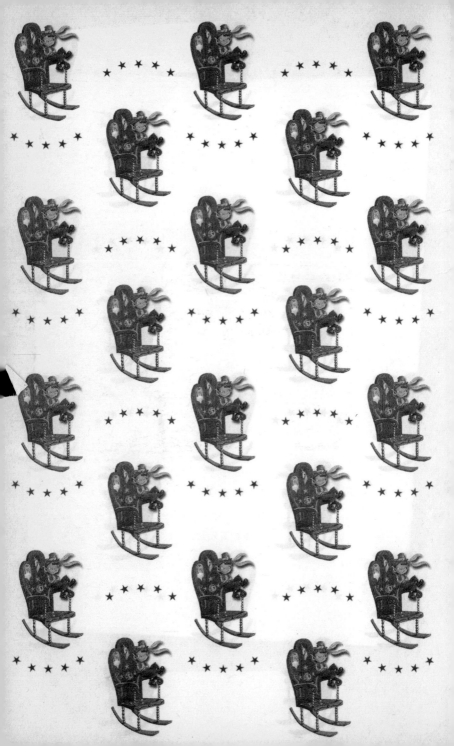

This book belongs to:

\- - - - - - - - - - - - - - - - - - - -

\- - - - - - - - - - - - - - - - - - - -

# Enid Blyton's
## The NEW Adventures of the
# Wishing~Chair

# The Land of Fairytales

## Illustrated by Erica-Jane Waters

**EGMONT**

*The New Adventures of the Wishing-Chair: The Land of Fairytales*
first published in Great Britain 2009
by Egmont UK Limited
239 Kensington High Street
London W8 6SA

Text and illustrations ENID BLYTON® copyright © 2009
Chorion Rights Limited. All rights reserved.
Illustrations by Erica-Jane Waters

The moral rights of the author and illustrator have been asserted

ISBN 978 1 4052 4391 9

1 3 5 7 9 10 8 6 4 2

www.egmont.co.uk

A CIP catalogue record for this title is available
from the British Library

Printed and bound in Great Britain by Clays Ltd, St Ives plc

# Contents

# The Characters

Jack

Jessica

Wishler

Daisy

**Storyteller**

**Thumbelina and Tom Thumb**

**Puss in Boots**

**Fairy Godmother**

# Chapter One

'And they all lived happily ever after,' Wishler read aloud. *'The End.'*

As Wishler closed the big, colourful book of fairytales, Jack and Jessica broke into loud applause. The pixie jumped to his feet and took a bow,

sweeping off his jaunty green hat with a flourish.

'That was brilliant, Wishler,' Jessica sighed happily. She got up from her stool and ran over to give him a hug. 'Thank you for reading all those stories.'

'You're very welcome.' Wishler's pointy face broke into a smile as he

placed the book on the floor.

Jessica, Jack and Wishler were
in the shed at the bottom of the
back garden of their house. Soon

after they'd moved to the village of Noware, Jack and Jessica had asked their parents' permission to turn the shed into a den. But what they *hadn't* told their mum and dad was that the shed was also a home for their very special, secret friend, Wishler the pixie. And this wasn't the children's only secret. Hidden

away in the shed with Wishler was a wonderful wishing-chair that took them on many exciting adventures.

'Wouldn't it be great if we could meet all those fairytale characters?' Jessica sighed.

'Well, we *could*,' Wishler said, his eyes twinkling, 'if we visit Fairyvale!'

'Fairyvale?' Jack and Jessica

repeated together.

Wishler nodded. 'It's the place where fairytales grow,' he replied. 'I've never been there myself, but I know it's where all the fairytale characters like Red Riding Hood and Snow White live.'

Jessica could hardly believe her ears. 'That sounds like a brilliant

place to visit, doesn't it, Jack?'

But Jack wasn't listening. Instead he was staring at the wooden wishing-chair in the corner of the shed, his eyes wide with delight. 'Look!' Jack shouted. 'The paintings on the wishing-chair are changing!'

Jack, Jessica and Wishler all rushed closer to see. They knew that

whenever the paintings started
to swirl and shift, it meant
the wishing-chair was

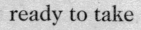

ready to take

them on

another fantastic

adventure.

'I can see

pumpkins, mice,

red apples
and a tall
beanstalk,' Jack
went on, pointing
out the pictures to
Jessica and Wishler.

'They're all things in the stories Wishler just read to us.'

'I think the chair wants to take us to Fairyvale!' Jessica guessed. 'I hope I get to meet Cinderella.'

'Let's go right away,' said Wishler.

The three friends sat down on the wishing chair's wooden seat and began to rock back and forth. As

they did so, bright blue sparks began to flash and fizz all around them.

'Take us to Fairyvale!' Jack, Jessica and Wishler shouted loudly on the third rock.

## Chapter Two

There was a dazzling flash of blue light and Jack and Jessica shut their eyes. A moment later they felt their feet touch down on a soft surface.

Jack opened his eyes first. 'We're in a wood!' he exclaimed, staring at

the enormous trees that surrounded them. 'Maybe we'll meet Red Riding Hood.'

'As long as we don't meet the Big Bad Wolf,' Jessica said nervously. In a clearing just up ahead of them, she spotted a small house, half hidden by trees. 'I wonder who lives in that sweet little house over there?'

Jessica saw Jack and Wishler turn to gaze at the house as well. But to her surprise, Jack took one look at her and burst out laughing.

'What's so funny?' she demanded.

'Have you *seen* what you're wearing?' Jack asked.

Jessica looked down at herself and gasped in surprise. When they'd left

home, she'd been wearing jeans and a purple sweatshirt. Now she was wearing a tattered blue dress covered in sooty stains.

'Well, look at what *you're* wearing, Jack,' Jessica said, raising her eyebrows. Her brother stopped laughing and gave a start of surprise as he realised that his grey T-shirt and

jeans had been magically replaced by a white shirt, green breeches and red boots.

'What's happened to our clothes, Jessica?' Jack asked. He turned to Wishler and looked the pixie up and down. 'And look! Your outfit has changed too.'

Wishler was now wearing a ragged

blue coat, red trousers and a battered black hat.

'What's going on, Wishler?' Jessica asked the pixie.

Wishler scowled fiercely at them. 'Oh, *do* be quiet!' he snapped.

Jack and Jessica looked at each other in amazement. Jessica was just about to ask why Wishler was being

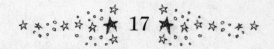

so irritable, when Jack gave a yell.

'Hang on! Where's the wishing-chair?' he asked. 'It's not here. It's vanished!'

'We were *standing up* when we arrived,' Jessica said. 'Usually we arrive sitting on the chair.'

'And then the chair disguises itself to fit in with wherever we've landed,'

Jack added. 'It's never disappeared before.'

'We *have* to find it,' Jessica said, determined. 'It's our only way home. Maybe it's inside that little house in the clearing?'

Wishler immediately dashed off towards the house without saying a word to Jack or Jessica.

'That's funny,' Jack murmured as they hurried through the trees after the pixie. 'Wishler always looks after us whenever we visit new places. He *never* leaves us on our own.'

'Maybe he's just worried about the wishing-chair,' Jessica suggested.

As they got closer to the house, Jack frowned. This didn't look like

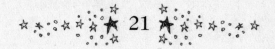

any *ordinary* house. And there was a strong, sweet smell in the air that made him think of Christmas.

'It's a *gingerbread* house!' he gasped, staring at the brown, spongy walls. Then he realised that the doorway was framed by red and white striped candy-canes and the window panes were moulded from

pink marzipan. The gingerbread walls were decorated with many coloured jelly-beans, and the roof was dusted with white icing sugar. Large red, yellow and green stripy lollipops lined the path that led to the front door and Wishler was standing at the beginning of it.

'There's only one gingerbread

house in fairytales that I've heard of,' Jessica said. 'And it belongs to the witch in *Hansel and Gretel*.'

'Let's hope our chair isn't inside,' replied her brother. 'I don't want to meet a wicked witch!'

Suddenly Wishler giggled and, to Jack and Jessica's astonishment, he leapt upwards as if he had springs

in his heels. With just one bound

he landed on the gingerbread roof,

sending up a fine mist of icing-sugar

like snow.

'Wishler, what are you doing?' Jack called.

Jessica stared up at Wishler. The pixie's face was all screwed up and he didn't look the least bit friendly. *What's the matter with him*, she wondered.

'Ha, ha, ha,' Wishler chuckled,

waving his hand in the air. 'I've got something you really, *really* want!'

Jack and Jessica stared at the strange brown shape that Wishler was now holding above his head.

'It looks a bit like a piece of gingerbread,' Jack said, puzzled.

Suddenly Jessica realised what it was. 'It *is* gingerbread, Jack – but

it's in the shape of a chair!' she cried. 'Wishler's found the wishing-chair. It must have disguised itself to fit with the house.'

'Well done, Wishler,' Jack called to their friend. 'Please bring the chair down, and we can hide it before we go exploring.'

But Wishler shook his head. 'You

can't have it,' he declared. 'It's mine and I'm keeping it!'

As Jack and Jessica watched, Wishler ran to the edge of the roof and somersaulted off it like a champion gymnast. Cackling loudly, he landed neatly on the grass and instantly disappeared amongst the thick trees of the wood.

## Chapter Three

'What's happened to Wishler?' Jessica said, horrified. 'He's not acting like himself at all!'

'I don't know,' Jack replied. 'But whatever's going on, we *have* to get the wishing-chair back or we'll never

make it home again. Come on!'

Jessica and Jack raced after Wishler through the trees. After a few moments, they noticed a bright light ahead of them. A couple of seconds later they burst out of the wood and into a beautiful green meadow, filled with dazzling golden sunshine.

Suddenly Jack stopped, and Jessica

 31

heard him gasp in awe.

'What is it, Jack?' Jessica cried. 'Is it Wishler?'

'No,' Jack replied in a dazed voice. 'Look there.' He pointed to his left. 'It's an *enormous* beanstalk!'

To her amazement, Jessica saw a huge plant standing in the meadow just ahead of them. The bright green stem of the plant was thicker than a tree trunk, and its glossy leaves were the biggest Jessica had ever seen. She gazed upwards. The beanstalk was so tall it disappeared out of sight into the big, fluffy clouds that dotted the sky.

A white cow stood in the meadow next to the beanstalk, grazing on the

grass. It mooed loudly, and Jessica smiled. The cow looked tiny next to the huge plant – rather like a toy farmyard animal! Right at that moment Jessica caught a glimpse of some red trousers across the meadow, out of the corner of her eye. 'Quick, Jack,' she called. 'I see Wishler!' She hurried towards

the open gate that led into the

next meadow.

But Jack stayed exactly where

he was.

'Jack, come on!' Jessica called, but she could see that her brother was mesmerized by the beanstalk.

'I have to climb it,' Jack shouted, moving towards the beanstalk. 'I don't know why, but I just *have* to climb it.'

'Jack, wait, please!' Jessica called out in alarm.

But Jack took no notice. Hauling himself up, he balanced his feet on the thick stems of the bottom leaves and began to climb.

Chapter
*Four*

'Jack!' Jessica shouted again. 'Come down from that beanstalk now.' Then she realised what she'd said. '*Jack*,' Jessica repeated to herself. '*Beanstalk*.' Then she let out a groan. 'Of course!'

Jack was still climbing steadily up the thick stem, a determined look on his face.

'Jack, I think you've become the *other* Jack,' Jessica called. 'The one from the fairytale. That's why you've got new clothes, and that's why you want to climb the beanstalk. You must fight the urge and come down!'

But to Jessica's dismay, Jack ignored her and kept climbing.

'Come down at once, Jack!' someone else shouted from behind Jessica.

She turned to meet the soft brown eyes of the cow.

'Before you ask, yes, that *was* me speaking,' the cow mooed.

Jessica tried to swallow down her amazement and looked back up at her brother. To her relief, she saw that Jack had stopped climbing. He was peering down at the talking cow, looking very surprised.

'There's really no point in you climbing up there,' the cow called. 'A naughty pixie has already stolen

the golden goose from the giant and run off.'

'A naughty pixie?' Jessica said with dismay. 'Wishler!' She looked up and saw that her brother's face was scrunched up with disappointment. Mumbling something under his breath he climbed back down the beanstalk carefully.

'I don't know *what's* going on with this story,' the cow went on with a sigh as Jack touched the ground. 'I'm Daisy, the other Jack's cow, and *he's* the one that's supposed to steal the golden goose from the giant's castle. There certainly isn't meant to be a pixie in *our* fairytale!'

'What am I going to do now that

someone else has taken the golden goose?' Jack wailed.

'You can snap out of it and help me find Wishler!' Jessica told him. 'Remember, this isn't actually your story.'

'You're absolutely right.' Jack shook his head as if he was trying to clear his thoughts.

'Jump on my back and we'll go after him,' Daisy urged them. 'I need to get the goose back and I saw the pixie go through that gate and into the next meadow.' She knelt down and Jack and Jessica climbed on to her broad, soft back. Daisy then trotted off surprisingly quickly and soon cantered through the open gate.

'I can't see Wishler anywhere,'
Jack said, glancing around. 'Can you,
Jessica?' His sister shook her head.

'I see something,' Daisy mooed excitedly. 'Look, over there, by the hedgerow.'

The cow trotted across the meadow. Ahead of them, Jack and Jessica saw a handsome black and white cat standing on his hind legs. He wore a smart blue coat and black breeches, and a large hat with a plumy white

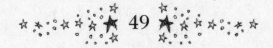

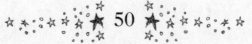

feather stuck in the side of it.

Jessica recognised him straight away. 'Excuse me, but are you Puss in Boots?' she asked eagerly.

The cat looked very sad. 'Well, I *was*,' he replied. 'But now I'm Puss *without* Boots. A horrible pixie has just stolen my brand-new shoes!'

'Oh dear, Wishler strikes again.

Why is he being so mean?' Jessica asked.

'I don't know,' Jack replied. 'But we've definitely got to find out before Wishler causes any more trouble.'

## Chapter
# *Five*

'You'd better come along with us, Puss,' Daisy said kindly. 'There's plenty of room.'

The cat hopped up on to Daisy's back behind Jack and Jessica, and they set off again.

'Which way did Wishler go?' asked Jessica.

'He followed that cobblestone path across the meadow,' Puss explained, pointing to a path that went through the grass and into the distance.

'Let's go, Daisy!' Jack cried.

Daisy trotted off as fast as possible along the path. The cobbled trail led

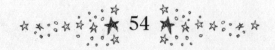

them through three more meadows
and over a little wooden bridge that
crossed a narrow, bubbling stream.
Then Daisy came to a sudden halt at
a fork in the path.

'Which way do you think your pixie
friend went?' Daisy asked.

'Right,' said Jessica.

'No, left,' said Jack.

'Maybe we'd better toss a coin to decide,' Puss suggested.

'I can help you!' called a very tiny voice.

'Who's that?' Jack asked, looking around.

'I don't know, but it sounded like it came from down *there*,' Jessica replied, pointing at the ground.

Jack, Jessica and Puss peered down from Daisy's back, and saw a tiny, golden-haired girl perched on a buttercup.

'Oh!' Jessica gasped, thinking back to the book of fairytales. 'Are you Thumbelina?'

The girl nodded. 'I am. And I know where that pixie was heading,' she said breathlessly. 'He just stole my best friend, Tom Thumb!'

Jessica leant down and carefully scooped Thumbelina up in her hand.

'Which way
did he
go?' she asked.

'That way!'
Thumbelina cried, pointing to the
right hand fork. 'Hurry!'

Daisy cantered off again, with
Thumbelina riding on Puss's shoulder.
They followed the path a bit further

and then, as they rounded a corner, they saw a huge manor house just ahead of them. The house had a large, open courtyard with a stone fountain set in the middle.

'Stop, Daisy!' Jessica shouted.

'What is it?' Jack asked as his sister leapt off the cow's back. 'Have you seen Wishler?' But Jessica didn't

answer. She ran down the path and straight into the courtyard without even looking back.

'What's going on?' Jack asked himself. Then he noticed a big orange pumpkin lying on the stone floor of the courtyard and six tiny white mice scampering round it. Beside them stood a woman in a flowing

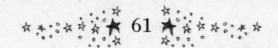

blue dress covered with sparkles.

She had glittering wings and

carried a wand topped with a golden

star. The woman smiled at his sister

and gave her a big hug.

'Jessica!' Jack jumped

down from Daisy's

back and ran into

the courtyard.

'What are you doing?'

He was just in time to hear the woman declare, 'Welcome my dear, I am your Fairy Godmother!'

'Oh, no,' Jack breathed, as Daisy, Puss, and Thumbelina joined him. 'Jessica's turning into Cinderella, just like I became Jack from *Jack and the Beanstalk*.'

Before

Jack could

say any

more, the

Fairy Godmother

waved her wand over Jessica's

head. Golden sparkles rained down

on her, and the next moment

Jessica's old tattered dress vanished,

and she was wearing a long silvery

ball gown and glass slippers.

Another wave of the magic wand

turned the pumpkin into a golden

coach, and the mice

into six beautiful white horses, who tossed their silky manes and pawed at the ground.

'Oh look, I *am* going to the ball,' Jessica announced, clapping her hands in delight. 'And I'm going to meet a prince!'

'No, you're not, Jessica,' Jack said, grabbing her hand. 'You can't go to

the ball – we have to find Wishler.'

'Ha, ha, ha!'

The sound of cackling made Jack and Jessica jump, and the next moment Wishler sprang out from behind a tall shrub and dashed across the courtyard.

'Wishler!' Jack cried. He stared at his friend in horror. Wishler's nose had become very long and sharp.

His ears had grown too and now

they stuck out from his head. But

most frightening

of all, his

skin had

turned

swamp

green.

The pixie had the golden goose tucked under one arm, and it was squawking loudly. As Wishler ran past Jack and Jessica, a tiny head popped out of his waistcoat pocket and shouted, 'Help!'

'It's Tom Thumb!' Thumbelina shouted from Daisy's back.

'And the pixie's wearing my new

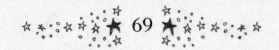

boots!' Puss pointed to the black leather boots on Wishler's feet.

'Wishler!' Jessica picked up her long skirt and ran after him. 'You *must* give back all the things you've stolen –'

But the pixie just cackled even more loudly. 'Wishler is not my name,' he yelled, 'and you'll *never*

find out my real one!'

Grinning all over his green face, Wishler jumped up on to the front of the golden coach that had been conjured up by the Fairy Godmother. He then flicked the reins and immediately the six white horses galloped fast out of the courtyard, pulling the carriage behind them.

## Chapter Six

'After him!' Puss shouted, waving his
hat in the air.

But Wishler and the golden carriage
had already vanished across the
meadow in a cloud of dust.

'I'm afraid you won't catch him

now, my dears,' the Fairy Godmother sighed. 'Those horses are *so* fast.'

'Maybe you could help us with your magic, Fairy Godmother?' Jack suggested eagerly.

But the Fairy Godmother shook her head. 'The pixie's not part of my story, so my magic won't work,' she explained. 'But I know someone who *can* help . . .'

Lifting her wand, she pointed to a tall tree a little way off. Jack and Jessica saw a man sitting down, leaning against the trunk. He was wearing a green velvet cape and a large, floppy, green hat.

'Well, come on then,' Jack said, and ran towards the mysterious man.

The others followed.

As they got closer, Jack saw that the man had an enormous gilded notebook spread open on his lap. A quill pen made from a golden feather was lying on top of it.

The man looked up from the pages of the book and his face broke into a smile. 'Hello, dear friends!' he called.

He placed the notebook carefully down on the grass and then jumped to his feet. 'I am the Storyteller,' the

man said, throwing his arms open wide. 'Helper and friend of every fairytale character in every story, and many others as well. How can I help you?'

'I'm Jack,' Jack said.

'And I'm Cinderella of course,' Jessica finished.

The Storyteller looked Jessica up

and down and frowned. 'No you're not. You're a *real* child who has been brought here by magic.'

Jack saw his sister blink rapidly, and smiled in relief as he heard her say, 'Oh, yes. Of course I am. My name is Jessica.'

The storyteller grabbed his quill and wrote some words in the air with a flourish.

*Welcome to Fairyvale!*

Everyone,

including Jack

and Jessica, gasped in wonder as

the words 'Welcome to

Fairyvale!'

appeared in

glittery golden

letters. They

hung in the air for a few seconds before fading into a shining mist.

'We came with our friend, Wishler,' Jessica explained carefully. 'He always comes with us whenever our wishing-chair brings us on a new adventure. But Wishler has changed since we arrived – he's stealing things from all the fairytales. We simply

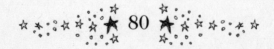

*must* find him.'

'Did you say his name is Wishler?' The Storyteller frowned. 'That doesn't sound like a child's name.'

'Oh, Wishler isn't a child,' Jack said. 'He's a pixie.'

'A pixie!' the Storyteller exclaimed in horror. 'But a pixie is a magical being, and they should *never* visit

Fairyvale. Their own magic makes very odd things happen here.'

'We didn't know that,' Jack said, glancing at Jessica in dismay.

The Storyteller began to pace up and down.

'This is very serious,' he declared. 'We have to find Wishler and return everything to its proper story

right away. Otherwise fairytales everywhere will be ruined!'

Jessica gasped. 'That would be terrible!'

'And don't forget we won't be able to get home if we don't find him,' Jack reminded her. 'Wishler still has the wishing-chair.'

Jessica groaned. 'How are we going

to catch Wishler and then persuade him to give everything back?'

'Well, first we have to find out which fairytale character Wishler has become,' the Storyteller told her. 'Any ideas?'

There was silence as Jack, Jessica and their fairytale friends thought hard. Which character could Wishler

be? Jack tried to remember some of

the things Wishler had said or done

that might give him a clue. The pixie

had seemed very bad-tempered, and

he'd been really mean to them. And he'd also said that Wishler wasn't his name . . .

Jack let out a gasp of excitement and at exactly the same moment Jessica gave a shout.

'*Rumplestiltskin!*' they both yelled.

## Chapter
### Seven

'Clearly, great minds think alike!'
The Storyteller grabbed his pen
and wrote *'Well done!'* in the air as
the fairytale characters broke into
delighted applause.

Jack and Jessica grinned at each

other in relief.

'But what do we do now?' Jack asked the Storyteller.

'You must break the spell on your friend and say his fairytale name,' the Storyteller replied. 'And I know exactly where you can find Rumplestiltskin.' He pointed his quill pen across the meadow towards a

wood in the distance. 'He has a little hut there, hidden deep amongst the trees.'

'Will you take us there, Daisy?' asked Jessica. But the cow shook her head, looking very nervous.

'None of us *ever* go to that part of Fairyvale,' Daisy explained. 'Those woods are far too dark and scary!'

Puss, Thumbelina and the Fairy Godmother nodded together.

'I guess we're on our own, then,' Jack said to Jessica.

'Good luck!' called the Storyteller, waving his hat as they left.

Jack and Jessica hurried into the woods. As they walked through the trees, it became colder and darker with each step.

'This place is horrible,' Jessica said with a shiver.

'Even the trees look scary here!'

Jack whispered.

A moment later Jack and Jessica stopped dead in their tracks. They could hear a strange, high-pitched noise.

'What's that?' Jessica asked.

Jack listened. 'I think someone's singing,' he said. 'And it's coming from over there!'

Silently, Jack and Jessica hurried over to a nearby tree and peered round the trunk to see a large, grassy clearing. They could see Cinderella's carriage and horses standing next to a ramshackle little wooden hut. A fire was burning in the middle of the grass, and Wishler was dancing around it

while holding on tight to the golden

goose. All the while he sang a

croaky song:

'The golden goose belongs to me,

These new boots fit perfectly!

I stole the carriage and Tom Thumb too,

You can't catch me, I'm smarter than you!

You'll never guess, it's such a shame,

But Rumplestiltskin is my name!'

Jack and Jessica suddenly jumped out from behind the tree.

'Wishler!' Jack called.

The pixie spun round and scowled at them.

'You need to give back everything you've stolen, Wishler,' Jessica said angrily. 'And we want the wishing-chair too.'

Wishler cackled with laughter. 'I'll only return everything if you say my name,' he yelled, hopping from one foot to the other. 'And you don't know it!' Still laughing, he dashed over to the carriage.

'We *do* know your name!' Jack shouted.

Wishler froze, just as he was about

97

to leap up on to the driver's seat. He looked back at Jack and Jessica in surprise.

Jack didn't hesitate. 'Your name is Rumplestiltskin!' he shouted, loud and clear.

## Chapter
## *Eight*

Wishler gave a gasp. Then he swayed
from side to side as if he was going
to faint. Jack rushed over to steady
him and Jessica took the golden
goose into her arms.

'Look, the green colour's fading

from his skin,' Jack pointed out.

'And his nose and ears are shrinking,' Jessica added. 'We did it, Jack – we broke the spell!'

'What happened to me?' Wishler asked weakly, opening his eyes. 'I had a terrible nightmare. I dreamt I was being really mean – and that I was bright green!'

'You turned into Rumplestiltskin,' Jack explained. 'But you're OK now.'

Suddenly a tiny head popped out from Wishler's pocket. 'Is it safe to come out?' asked Tom Thumb.

Wishler jumped and stared at Tom in surprise. 'Yes, it's quite safe,' he said after a moment, looking a bit red and embarrassed.

'Come on, it's time to go back to the Storyteller.' Jessica opened the carriage door and helped Wishler inside. She sat the golden goose next to them, as Jack climbed into the driver's seat.

'Giddyup!' Jack shouted, shaking the reins, and the six horses galloped off.

In no time they were speeding
across the meadow towards the tree
where the Storyteller and the other
fairytale characters

were

waiting.

They all

cheered

as they

saw the coach racing towards them.

Jack halted the horses, and then

Jessica and Wishler climbed out.

'I'm so very sorry,' Wishler said,

looking very sheepish as he handed

the boots to Puss. 'Please forgive me,

all of you.'

'No hard feelings!' Puss purred,

offering a paw for Wishler to shake.

'But where's my Tom Thumb?'
Thumbelina called, as the golden
goose waddled out of the carriage
towards Daisy.

'Here I am!' a voice shouted, and Tom popped out of Wishler's pocket again. Jessica placed him carefully on the grass and the two tiny friends

hugged each other happily.

'Now Cinderella *shall* go to the ball!' the Fairy Godmother declared, patting one of the horses.

The Storyteller nodded. 'Yes, I'll put all the stories right, don't worry.'

Jessica sighed with relief. 'And we should be getting home,' she said, glancing at Wishler and Jack.

Wishler put his hand in his other pocket. Pulling out the gingerbread chair, he placed it on the grass. 'Show yourself!' he said tapping the chair, and instantly the wishing-chair appeared. The three friends piled on to the seat, calling

goodbye to the Storyteller and to the fairytale characters.

'This is a happy ending to your story my friends,' the Storyteller said with a smile. 'Jack, Jessica and Wishler,' he murmured softly. 'Yes, I shall have to find a use for those names. Goodbye!'

'Goodbye,' Puss and all the other

characters called as Jack, Jessica and Wishler began to rock the wishing-chair.

'I suppose my beautiful dress will vanish now,' Jessica sighed, stroking the silver material. 'I didn't meet Cinderella after all, but at least I got to wear her ball gown.'

'Home!' Jack shouted.

There was a flash of sparkling blue light. And when it cleared, Jack, Jessica and Wishler found that they were back in the shed.

'Oh, we're ourselves again,' Jessica said, looking down at her sweatshirt and jeans.

Then Jack pointed at the book of fairytales which they'd left lying on

the shed floor.

'Look!' he gasped excitedly. 'The book is glowing!'

The book was casting a golden light around the shed. Quickly Jack leafed through it. 'There's a new story at the back!' he announced.

'*Adventures In Fairyvale*,' Jessica read out over Jack's shoulder. She

pointed at a page inside the book. 'Look, there are drawings of *us*. And I'm wearing Cinderella's dress!'

'Let's read the story,' Wishler suggested eagerly.

They sat down with their backs against the wall of the shed, Jessica in the middle. She read out the entire fairytale to the end.

'So the travellers returned to their home,' Jessica finished. 'But they had many other adventures with the wishing-chair, each one more wonderful than the last. And they lived happily ever after!'

## EGMONT PRESS: ETHICAL PUBLISHING

Egmont Press is about turning writers into successful authors and children into passionate readers – producing books that enrich and entertain. As a responsible children's publisher, we go even further, considering the world in which our consumers are growing up.

**Safety First**
Naturally, all of our books meet legal safety requirements. But we go further than this; every book with play value is tested to the highest standards – if it fails, it's back to the drawing-board.

**Made Fairly**
We are working to ensure that the workers involved in our supply chain – the people that make our books – are treated with fairness and respect.

**Responsible Forestry**
We are committed to ensuring all our papers come from environmentally and socially responsible forest sources.

**For more information, please visit our website at www.egmont.co.uk/ethical**

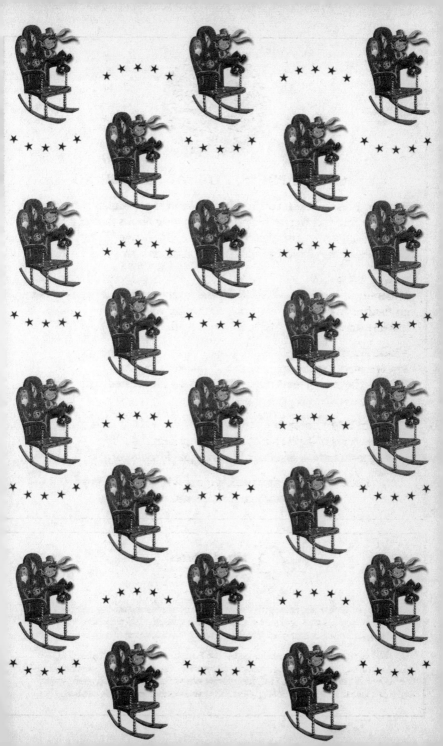

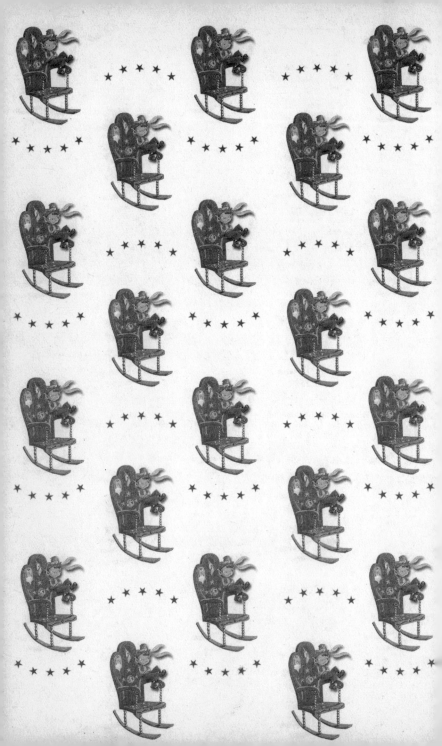